FRANKLIN and LUNA
GO TO THE MOON

JEN CAMPBELL • KATIE HARNETT

Thames & Hudson

Luna loves stories.
Stories make her world feel bright.

She reads exciting adventures all night long,
curled up with her tortoise, Neil Armstrong.

Luna has a best friend called Franklin.
Franklin isn't like her other friends at all.

He is ... larger.
He is ... greener.

And sometimes, when they are playing board games,
he accidentally sneezes fluorescent blue flames.

Luna and Franklin want to be explorers,
and visit the places they've read about in books.

They've practised map reading
and even tried speaking
in Mermish and Gibberish and Gobbledegook.

They've read about mermaids and harpies and selkies,
magical creatures that live in the wild.

They've learned that fairies are naughty.
Ghosts are quite clumsy.

Werewolves take holidays by the seaside.

'And dragons?' asks Luna. 'Where do they hide?'

'I don't remember,' Franklin says. 'I haven't seen any others.
I've been searching a while, I'm six hundred and five!'

'But where is your family? What's their address?'

Franklin pauses for thought. He scratches his head.

'I've got a third cousin who lives in Loch Ness.
I've been sending her letters with little success.'

Luna suggests they go on an adventure
to search for Franklin's family and explore the world together!

On their journey they find ...

Twenty yetis eating spaghetti.

    Five vampires reading Shakespeare.

Two giants playing chess

       and poltergeists in fancy dress.

Elves playing volleyball.
    Nymphs with skipping ropes.
Tiny pixies throwing frisbees
        under microscopes.

Tooth fairies in ice cream vans.
    Witches baking cherry pie.
        Disco dancing unicorns
on roller skates – oh my!

Franklin and Luna collapse in a heap.

They've looked high and low and in between
and now they've got sore feet.

They've Googled Franklin's family tree.
They've emailed a princess.
But no one knows where dragons live, no one can even guess!

Except ...

Neil Armstrong clears his throat and points way up high.
Luna grabs her telescope and peers at the sky.

Something moving far away can't help but catch her eye.

Luna tickles Franklin's nostrils
to try and make him sneeze.

'A-A-ATCHOO!'

Bright blue flames shoot out his nose,
and lift them up with speed.

They zoom up in the air at an exhilarating pace.
Through all the clouds and out again ...

... they rocket into space!

They pass shooting stars and spaceships,
unsure which way to go …

It's dark and cold and endless.
Perhaps they should go home?

But … wait! Franklin's starting to remember this place from long ago.
'I recall that constellation! And that galaxy!

I used to fly here as a young dragon,
when I was a hundred and forty three!'

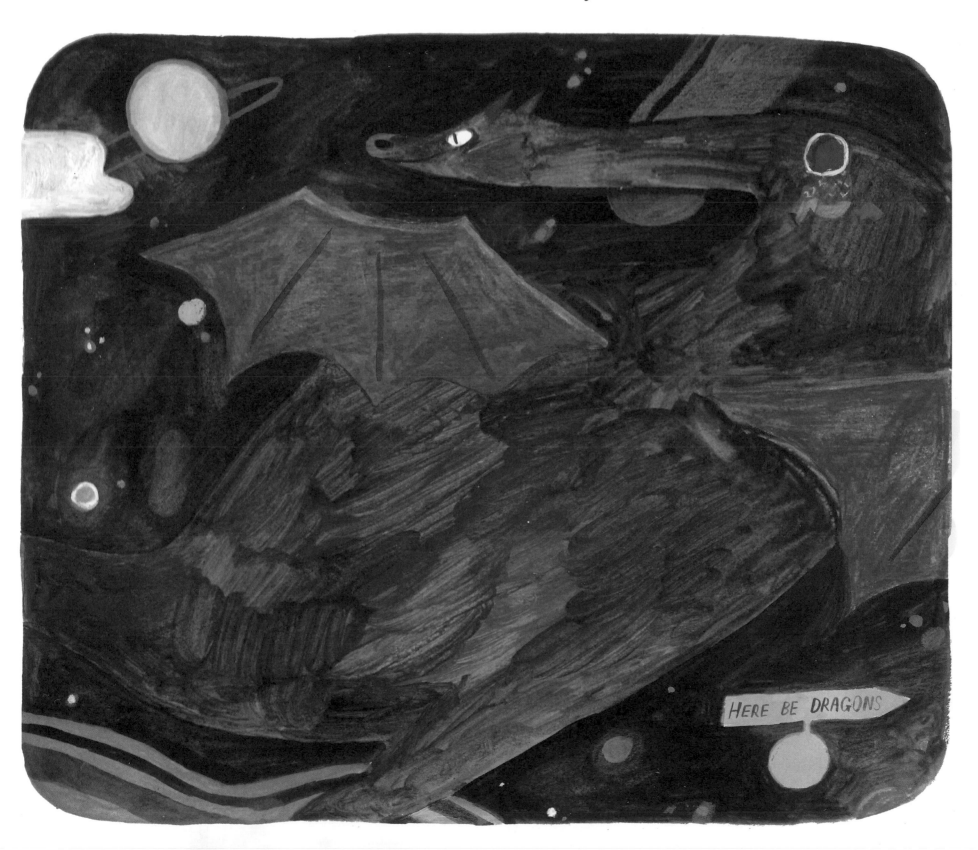

Luna, Franklin and Neil Armstrong collide with the surface of the moon.

There are craters full of libraries
and glowing midnight flowers.
Glitter falling onto them
from meteor showers.

'Hello?' Franklin calls.
His voice echoes on the air.

All is quiet.
All is silent.

No dragons anywhere.

They set off to explore
through a forest of ghostly trees.

They pass a milky ocean

and swarms of sleepy bees.

In the sand, they spy some footprints.
Franklin hears a familiar song.
Slowly, he remembers: 'I think this is where I'm from!'

They hurry towards the music and stumble upon ...

... dozens of silver dragons with moon dust on their scales
playing board games and ice skating and reading fairy tales.

'Look! A human!' yells a dragon.

'They're so scary,' another says.

'Don't worry,' Franklin jumps in.
'This is Luna. She's my friend.'

'Franklin, is that you?' they gasp.
They hug him tight with glee
and Franklin's reunited with his long lost family.

'We always hoped you'd visit!'
'We're so glad that you're here!'
'We sent letters using shooting stars.'
'We thought you'd disappeared!'

Franklin tells his family about his home below,
about all the different people
and all the places you can go.

Franklin's cousin teaches Luna how to sing dragon songs,
how to play space hockey
and bake stardust scones.

All together, they share stories, sitting beneath the stars.
They giggle and take photographs, they talk for many hours ...

... about family trees, and they all agree this reunion has been such fun.
They shouldn't wait four hundred years to have another one!

Luna's given lots of books so she can learn about the moon,
and Franklin's cousin promises
she'll come to see them very soon.

When it's time to go home
they hug goodbye
and hand Franklin a map ...

... so that when they want to visit
they can always travel back.

'For Ollie and Phoebe' – Jen Campbell
'For my family' – Katie Harnett

First published in the United Kingdom in 2018 by Thames & Hudson Ltd,
181A High Holborn, London WC1V 7QX

First paperback edition 2019

Franklin and Luna Go to the Moon © 2018 Thames & Hudson Ltd, London

Illustrations © 2018 Katie Harnett
Text by Jen Campbell

British Library Cataloguing-in-Publication Data
A catalogue record for this book is available from the British Library

ISBN 978-0-500-65217-6

Printed and bound in China through Asia Pacific Offset Ltd

To find out about all our publications, please visit **www.thamesandhudson.com**.
There you can subscribe to our e-newsletter, browse or download our
current catalogue, and buy any titles that are in print.